MERCER MAYER'S
LC + THE CRITTER KIDS®

TOP DOG

A Golden Book • New York

Western Publishing Company, Inc., Racine, Wisconsin 53404

A Mercer Mayer Ltd./J. R. Sansevere Book

Library of Congress Catalog Card Number: 93-80455
ISBN: 0-307-15981-7/ISBN: 0-307-65981-X (lib. bdg.) A MCMXCIV

Written by Erica Farber/J. R. Sansevere
For Ruby Tuesday

CN
far

LC

VELVET

LITTLE SISTER

TIGER

KOOL BEAR

SLICK RICK

SU SU   GABBY   TIMOTHY

GATOR   FLEX   HENRIETTA

CHAPTER 1

LC AT BAT

LC went flying around the corner. He ran as fast as he could down the block. He had to get to Critter Comics. It was Friday afternoon, when all the new comics came in. He skidded to a stop in front of the store and rushed inside.

"Is it in yet?" LC asked Mr. Marvel. "Is the new *X-Critter* in yet?"

"Yes, LC, it's over there with the new comics," said

Mr. Marvel. He pointed to a display at the front of the store.

LC hurried over to the display. He picked up a copy of the *X-Critter* comic. He had to have it. As a matter of fact, he had to have two copies—one to read and one to add to his collection.

LC stuck his hand in his pocket to check that he still had his ten-dollar bill. It was the most money that he had ever had all at once. It was a surprise present from his Uncle Andy. Uncle Andy's card had said, "Don't spend it all in one place." But Uncle Andy didn't know how many cool things there were to buy at Critter Comics. LC was sure Uncle Andy would change his mind if he knew.

Just then LC noticed that the new *Spider Critter* comic was there. He had to have two of those, too. LC held on tightly to the four comics, when he suddenly saw the new *Super Silver Critter* comic. He

definitely had to have that as well.

LC brought all the comics over to the counter. He put his stack down right next to the display of the new Critter Club basketball cards. LC really wanted the Shack O. Critter card. Shack was the hottest rookie and jammer. The card was worth more than one-hundred dollars. He knew there weren't many Shack cards out there, but maybe he'd be lucky and get one if he bought a pack.

Mr. Marvel started to add up how much all of LC's comics cost. The grand total came to nine dollars and fifty cents. LC fingered his ten-dollar bill.

"I have just enough left for a pack of Critter Club cards," said LC. "So I'll take one of those."

"Are you sure you want to spend all of your money, LC?" Mr. Marvel asked, raising his eyebrows. "Do you really need two copies of each comic?"

"Yes, yes," said LC. "I always rip the ones I read. So I need to have another copy to put away."

"Well, couldn't you be more careful then?" asked Mr. Marvel. "You'd save yourself a lot of money. And anyway, you ought to save some money for a rainy day."

"Why would I need money for a rainy day?" asked LC.

"It's just a saying," said Mr. Marvel. "It

means you ought to save your money in case something happens."

"Like what?" asked LC.

"That's just it," said Mr. Marvel. "You never know what might happen, or when it's going to be a rainy day."

LC looked out the window. The sun was shining. It looked like it would never rain. "That's okay, Mr. Marvel," said LC. "I don't think it's going to rain. I'll take everything."

Mr. Marvel put LC's comics and pack of cards in a bag.

"Thanks, Mr. Marvel," said LC. He grabbed the bag and hurried out of the store. He had no time to lose. He was supposed to meet the Critter Kids to play baseball. But he had to go home first to get his mitt.

LC ran home. He barged through the back door into the kitchen. His mother was baking cookies with Little Sister. The door slammed shut behind him, making Mrs. Critter and Little Sister jump.

"Hello, LC," said his mother. "Why are you in such a big hurry?"

"I'm late for the baseball game," said LC. "Have you seen my mitt?" He walked over to the table and grabbed a cookie. He shoved the whole thing into his mouth. Then he took another one.

"No, I haven't," said Mrs. Critter. "If you put your things away after you use them, you would know where your mitt is."

Yo Yo, LC's dog, snatched the cookie out of his hand and scurried out of the kitchen.

"How was school?" Mrs. Critter asked.

"Good," said LC, taking another cookie.

"What's in the bag?" asked Little Sister.

"Comics," mumbled LC through a mouthful of cookie. "I got all the coolest ones."

"I hope you didn't spend all the money Uncle Andy sent you," said Mrs. Critter.

"Mom put all my money in my bank account," said Little Sister. "I'm saving my money."

Just then Yo Yo came trotting back into the kitchen with LC's baseball mitt in his mouth. There were teeth marks all over it,

and the leather was chewed up.

"Give me that, Yo Yo," said LC, grabbing the mitt out of Yo Yo's mouth. "You destroyed my favorite mitt."

Yo Yo just looked at him and wagged his tail.

"Dumb dog," said LC, taking another cookie and heading for the door.

"Well, that's what happens when you don't put all of your things away," said Mrs. Critter. But LC didn't hear her. He was already halfway down the driveway with Yo Yo at his heels.

Tiger, Gabby, Gator, and Timothy were waiting for LC in the empty lot between Mrs. Crabtree's house and the corner.

"LC, you're up first," Tiger called as LC and Yo Yo ran onto the field. "Gabby, you're pitching. I've got second. Gator, you're on first, and Timothy, you're right field."

"Oh, no," Gabby said. "Yo Yo can't play. He'll wreck the game. Remember last time when he slobbered all over the ball and it got so slimy we couldn't even catch it?"

"Aw, come on," said LC. "Yo Yo's not so bad. Let him play left field. He won't bother anybody out there."

Yo Yo looked up at Gabby and wagged his tail. "Oh, all right," said Gabby. "Let's get started." Yo Yo jumped up and licked Gabby's face and then raced out to left field.

"Yuck!" Gabby said. "That dog is disgusting."

"He's just showing that he likes you," said LC.

"Gross," said Gabby, wiping her face with the bottom of her T-shirt as she walked over to the pitcher's mound. "A home run is over the fence in Mrs. Crabtree's yard," she said.

"This one's going over the fence," LC said as he walked up to the batter's box. He dug his feet into the dirt and got into his batting stance.

Gabby went into her windup. She threw

a fastball right up the middle.

LC kept his eyes glued to the ball. Just as it came over the plate, he swung as hard as he could. The ball went flying. LC ran toward first base. He was psyched. He knew he had hit a home run.

Timothy and Yo Yo raced toward the fence from opposite sides of the field. They bumped into each other and fell to the ground. The ball soared over the fence.

LC ran from first to second. Suddenly there was a loud crash, and LC stopped in his tracks.

"Uh-oh!" said Gabby. Everyone else stood with their mouths wide open.

"Who hit this ball through my window?" Mrs. Crabtree yelled. She was standing on her side porch, holding their baseball in her hand.

The Critter Kids looked at each other and slowly walked over to Mrs. Crabtree's fence.

"Which one of you nasty little critters did it?" she yelled.

No one said a word.

"You better tell me," Mrs. Crabtree said. "Because whoever did it is going to pay for my window."

"Sorry, Mrs. Crabtree," mumbled LC. "It was my fault."

"Well, then, Mr. Critter, you owe me twenty-five dollars," said Mrs. Crabtree.

"And I want the money by Sunday. Every last cent. Or else."

CHAPTER 2

DOLLARS AND SENSE

LC and the Critter Kids went across the street to LC's house. They sat down on the curb and stared at the ground. Yo Yo lay at LC's feet.

Just then Henrietta came riding down the street on her bicycle. She was delivering newspapers. "Extra, extra, read all about it!" Henrietta yelled. "Critterville Cat Burglar strikes again!"

She reached into her bag to throw one of the

newspapers into LC's yard. Yo Yo started
barking. He jumped up and ran as
Henrietta threw the paper. He leaped and
caught it in midair.

"Here, Yo Yo," LC called. "Bring me the
paper."

But Yo Yo wouldn't listen. He just ran in
circles around the yard.

"That dog is a real brat," said Gabby. "I
don't know how you put up with him."

"He's not so bad," said LC as Yo Yo came running by. LC tried to grab the paper, but Yo Yo wouldn't let go. He just kept on running.

Henrietta stopped in front of everybody. "Hey, did you hear about the cat burglar?" she asked.

"No," everybody said.

"What did he steal?" Gabby asked.

"Jewelry," said Henrietta, blowing a big

purple bubble with her gum. "Diamond jewelry. That's all he ever steals."

"Really?" gasped Gabby.

"Yep," said Henrietta. "It's his third break-in in three weeks. And the police haven't got a single clue."

Yo Yo brought the paper over to LC and dropped it at his feet.

"Well, I have to get back to my route," Henrietta said, blowing another bubble. "Gotta keep all of Critterville up on the latest about the cat burglar. See ya later."

With that, Henrietta hopped on her bike and pedaled away.

They watched her throw a paper into Mrs. Crabtree's yard. Yo Yo jumped up again and ran after it. He dashed into Mrs. Crabtree's yard and picked up the paper just as Mrs. Crabtree came out of her house.

"Shoo, shoo," Mrs. Crabtree said. She tried to take the paper from Yo Yo, but he wouldn't let go.

"Give me my paper," Mrs. Crabtree yelled. But Yo Yo just held on tight.

Mrs. Crabtree yanked on the other end of the paper with all of her might. Just then

Yo Yo let go and Mrs. Crabtree fell backward into a big mud puddle, splashing mud everywhere.

"You're going to pay for this!" Mrs. Crabtree yelled across her yard to the Critter Kids. "You and your mangy mutt of a dog!" Mrs. Crabtree wiped mud off her

nose as she slowly stood up. There was mud all over her shoes, all over her dress, and even on her hair.

"Yo Yo, get over here!" yelled LC. "Leave

Mrs. Crabtree alone." Yo Yo ran back across the street and dropped down at LC's feet. Then he stood up and shook, getting mud all over LC and his friends.

"That dog is a menace," said Gabby, wiping mud off her shorts.

"He doesn't mean to do anything bad," said LC. "Right, Yo Yo?"

Yo Yo looked up at LC and then lay down, putting his paws on LC's sneakers and getting mud all over them.

"How will I ever get Mrs. Crabtree her twenty-five dollars?" LC asked. He was so worried that he didn't even notice how muddy his sneakers were.

"Don't sweat it, dude," said Tiger.

"We're in it together," said Gabby.

"That's why we're the Critter Kids," said Tiger. "It's one for all and all for one." Tiger jumped up to do the Critter Kid Shake. He stood in front of LC and held out his hands. They double-slapped each other five, flapped elbows, grabbed each other's right hands, let go, and yelled, "Boom!"

"The Critter Kids are in the house!" Tiger yelled as Gabby, Gator, and Timothy jumped up to do the Shake.

"So, what are we going to do?" asked Gabby.

"I know," said Timothy. "Let's go to the clubhouse and see how much money we have in the treasury."

The Critter Kids walked over to the clubhouse. It was really an old barn that used to be the Critters' garage, but LC and his friends had made it into their clubhouse. Yo Yo followed them, carrying the newspaper.

The Critter Kids sat around the clubhouse table. Timothy picked up the coffee can that they used as their treasury and dumped the money out. There were four pennies, two nickels, and one quarter—a total of thirty-nine cents.

"What happened to all our money?" asked LC.

"I don't know," said Gabby. "What did we do with it?"

"We spent it on stuff," said Timothy, shaking his head. "As usual."

"Yeah," said Gator. "Remember last week when we had to buy those *Super Critter Collector Comics*?"

"Oh, yeah," said LC. He suddenly thought of what Mr. Marvel had told him. "We should have saved our money for a rainy day."

"But it's not raining," said Tiger, looking out the clubhouse window.

"It doesn't really mean raining," said LC. "It's just an old saying."

"It means saving your money in case of emergencies," said Timothy. "Because you never know what might happen."

"Well, now what?" asked Gabby. "We need way more money than thirty-nine cents."

"I know," said Tiger. "Let's look in the

newspaper. Maybe we can get a job."

The newspaper was lying on the floor at LC's feet, right in front of Yo Yo's nose. As soon as LC reached for the paper, Yo Yo grabbed it and ran outside. Everybody ran after Yo Yo.

"Give me the paper, Yo Yo," yelled LC.

Yo Yo just looked at him. LC grabbed hold of one end, but Yo Yo wouldn't let go. They both pulled, and the paper started to rip.

"You're going to wreck that paper," said Gabby.

"I'll get it," said LC. "Watch me. I'm going to use a special trick—I call it the 'Incredible Unbelievable Never-Failable Yo Yo Stopper.'"

"Right," said Gabby.

"That dog is out of control. You'll never get that paper away from him in one piece, with or without some special trick."

"Gabby's right," said Gator. "That dog is pretty tricky."

LC lay down on his stomach with his face in the grass. Yo Yo looked at him and then walked slowly toward him, the paper in his mouth. LC didn't move. Yo Yo sniffed LC's head. LC still didn't move. Yo Yo sat on LC's back. LC still didn't move. Suddenly LC rolled over and Yo Yo fell backward onto the grass next to him. LC began to tickle Yo Yo on his tummy. And that's when Yo Yo dropped the paper.

"Bingo!" said LC. "I told you it never fails."

Yo Yo ran to the other side of the yard.

He started digging a hole. Gabby opened the newspaper.

"Hey," LC said, looking over Gabby's shoulder. "The Critterville Dog Show is Sunday at the Town Hall. First prize is twenty-five dollars."

"That's exactly what we need to give Mrs. Crabtree," said Tiger.

"Yeah," agreed LC. "That's perfect."

"All we need is a dog," said Gator.

"Let's enter Yo Yo," said LC.

All eyes turned to Yo Yo. He was digging a big hole in Mr. Critter's prize flower bed.

"Forget Yo Yo," said Gabby. "He'll never win. We better look for a job."

"Yo Yo could win," said LC. "He just needs some training. Yo Yo, come here, boy," LC called.

Yo Yo ran across the yard. He dropped the flowers he'd dug up at LC's feet. Just then Mr. Critter came home from work. He was carrying his briefcase and a paper bag filled with groceries. Yo Yo dashed across the yard toward him.

"Back! Yo Yo, back!" yelled Mr. Critter, holding his briefcase in front of him as if it was a shield.

"What's he doing that for?" asked Tiger.

"'Cuz Yo Yo gets so excited to see him that he sometimes pees on his shoes," LC explained.

"Gross!" said Gabby.

As soon as Yo Yo got close to Mr. Critter,

he jumped up to grab the paper bag. Mr. Critter ran into the house and managed to shut the door without dropping the bag.

"That was close," said LC. "He doesn't always make it."

"What does Yo Yo want the bag for?" asked Gator.

"Because whenever we give him a biscuit it comes out of a paper bag," explained LC. "So he thinks all paper bags have biscuits in them."

"I told you that dog was a menace," said Gabby. "There is no way he'd ever make it into a dog show, let alone win one."

LC shrugged. Maybe Gabby was right, LC thought. Yo Yo was not exactly the show dog type. "I guess we should get a job," said LC.

"Definitely," said Gabby. "Tomorrow morning we should meet right after breakfast and go into town. That's where everybody goes to get jobs."

CHAPTER 3

TRICKS AND TREATS

LC got up early the next morning. He whistled as he got dressed. He didn't think getting a job was going to be a problem.

LC went into his parents' bedroom. "Mom, Dad," LC said, leaning against the doorway. "I'm going to town to get a job. I've decided that I need to make some money. You know, for a rainy day."

"What?" Mr. Critter said, sitting up in bed. "A rainy day?"

"Yeah," said LC. "Everybody should have money for a rainy day."

"That's a good idea, LC," said Mr. Critter. "But it may be harder than you think to get a job."

"Just be home in time for dinner," said Mrs. Critter. "And if you take Yo Yo, put him on his leash."

"No sweat," said LC. "See ya later."

LC slid down the banister and landed with a thud at the bottom of the stairs. Yo Yo looked up at him and wagged his tail.

"Where's your leash, boy?" LC asked.

Yo Yo just looked at him.

LC went into the kitchen and Yo Yo followed. LC didn't see Yo Yo's leash anywhere, but he had an idea. He opened one of the kitchen drawers and took out his dad's rope.

"Here, Yo Yo," LC said. "I'm going to make you a leash."

LC tied one end of the rope onto Yo Yo's collar and held on to the other end. "Let's go, Yo Yo," said LC. "We've got no time to lose."

LC and Yo Yo went flying out the back door and headed for town. Yo Yo knew the way and pulled LC along. When they got to Main Street, LC saw Gabby, Timothy, Gator, and Tiger waiting on the corner.

Even though there weren't any cars on the street, Yo Yo and LC waited for the light to change from red to green. They both checked for cars again and then dashed across the street.

"You're late, LC," Gabby said, stamping her foot. "And why did you bring that dog? We'll never get a job with that dog."

LC shrugged. Yo Yo hung his head.

"Well, we better get going," said Gabby. "I think our first stop should be Critter Sweet Treats."

Just then a police car came down the block with its lights flashing. It pulled up right in front of the Critter Kids.

They all froze. LC couldn't believe Mrs. Crabtree had already called the police. It wasn't even Sunday morning. The Critter Kids watched as Sergeant Pokey slowly got out of the police car and walked toward them.

LC held his hands up in the air, ready to

be handcuffed. "I did it," he said. "They're innocent."

But Sergeant Pokey walked right by LC and put up a poster on a lamppost.

"'*Wanted: Critterville Cat Burglar*,'" Timothy read out loud. "'*Twenty-five dollar reward*.'"

"Have a nice day," Sergeant Pokey said to the Kids as he got back into his car.

"Let's go," said Gabby.

Everybody followed Gabby down the block to Critter Sweet Treats. There was a sign in the window: HELP WANTED, EXPERIENCE REQUIRED.

"Perfect," said Gabby.

They walked inside. Yo Yo sneaked over to the candy area.

"Yum," said LC, licking his lips. "Maybe we should get some candy."

"Yeah," agreed Tiger.

"We're here for a job," said Gabby. "Not candy."

"Oh, right," Tiger and LC said.

"Can I help you?" Mr. Bear asked. He looked at the Kids and then at Yo Yo.

"Why, yes, you can," said Gabby. "We're here about the job."

"The job?" said Mr. Bear.

"Yeah, the one advertised in the window," said Gabby.

"Well, you need experience," said Mr. Bear, turning to look at Yo Yo again.

"We have lots of experience with candy," said LC.

"That's not the kind of experience I mean," said Mr. Bear. "Hey, your dog is eating my candy!"

The Critter Kids turned and watched as Yo Yo slipped another piece of chocolate into his mouth. There were wrappers lying all over the floor.

Mr. Bear walked over to Yo Yo. He

counted the empty wrappers. "That will cost you thirty-nine cents," said Mr. Bear.

Timothy took the club's money out of his pocket and handed it to Mr. Bear.

"Now, you kids better get that dog out of here before he eats any more candy," said Mr. Bear.

LC grabbed Yo Yo and pulled him outside. Everybody followed.

"We would have had that job if Yo Yo hadn't eaten that candy," said Gabby. "That dog is a real problem."

"Sorry," said LC. He and Yo Yo both stared at the ground.

"We better take him home before we look for any more jobs," said Gabby.

"I guess you're right," said LC.

The Critter Kids turned around and headed back to LC's house. Just as they got to the corner, they met Su Su. She was walking her dog.

"Sit, Princess," Su Su said. Princess sat.

"Wow!" said Tiger. "Your dog is really well trained."

"I know," said Su Su. "She just graduated from obedience school. She was top dog, and I'm going to enter her in the Critterville Dog Show. Princess and I are going to win first prize."

"How do you know you're going to win?" Gabby asked.

"Because Princess is top dog," said Su Su.

"Top dog?" said Gabby. "Why is she top dog?"

"Because she's perfect," said Su Su. "Just like me."

"Oh, please," said Gabby.

Yo Yo, who had been watching Princess, walked up to her and wagged his tail. Princess wagged back.

"Get that mutt away from my Princess," said Su Su to Gabby. "Princess is a purebred dog and I don't want her around any dogs that don't come from champion bloodlines."

"Let's go, Gabby," said LC. But Gabby wouldn't budge.

"This dog happens to be a champion,"

said Gabby. "I'm training him myself."

LC, Tiger, Timothy, and Gator all looked at each other.

Suddenly Yo Yo started running around and around. Princess started running around and around, too.

"Your dog is a bad dog!" yelled Su Su.

"Yo Yo!" called LC.

"Princess!" called Su Su.

But Yo Yo and Princess wouldn't listen. They just kept running around in circles. Yo Yo's rope wrapped around Su Su's legs and Su Su fell to the ground. Yo Yo licked Su Su's face.

"Gross!" said Su Su. "Get this dog off me. That's the worst dog I ever saw."

"Oh, yeah," said Gabby. "Just wait until we win first prize at the Critterville Dog Show."

LC stared at Gabby.

"Give me that leash," Gabby said. LC handed her the rope.

"Yo Yo, heel," Gabby said. But Yo Yo didn't pay any attention. He just ran ahead, pulling Gabby behind him.

LC smiled. He knew Yo Yo could be top dog. Like he had said, all Yo Yo needed was a little training.

CHAPTER 4

OBEDIENCE SCHOOL DROPOUT

That afternoon LC, Tiger, Gator, and Timothy were at the clubhouse. They were playing cards and Yo Yo was fast asleep, lying under the table.

"What are you guys doing?" Gabby asked as she walked inside. "You were supposed to give Yo Yo a bath before the training session."

"Shhhh," said LC. "Don't say that word."

Yo Yo started to slink out

from under the table.

"What word can't I say?" asked Gabby.

"The B-A-T-H word," said LC quietly.

"Oh, you mean BATH!" Gabby said loudly.

At that moment Yo Yo took off and ran out of the clubhouse as fast as he could go. The Critter Kids ran after him.

"Yo Yo!" LC called, but Yo Yo just barked and ran away. Yo Yo dashed across the yard, heading for Mrs. Crabtree's house.

"Oh, no. Look!" LC said. "Mrs. Crabtree is taking her groceries out of her car. And they're all in paper bags. . . ."

"We'll never make it over there fast enough," said Tiger.

"Forget it. It's too late," said Gabby. "He just jumped over the fence."

"Oh, no," muttered LC. "Not again."

"Let's go," said Timothy. They all took off across the yard after Yo Yo, but he kept on running. He didn't stop until he collided with Mrs. Crabtree, just as she pulled another bag of groceries out of her car. She dropped the bag, and everything inside it crashed to the ground. Just as the Critter Kids ran up her front walk, she slipped on a banana and landed in a gushy mush of broken eggs and spilled milk.

"Get this dog out of here!" yelled Mrs. Crabtree, trying to stand up and slipping again.

"Sorry, Mrs. Crabtree," said LC, holding out his hand to help her up. "It was an accident."

Mrs. Crabtree reached for LC's hand, just as Yo Yo jumped on him, making him lose his balance. LC tried to grab Mrs. Crabtree,

but it was too late. She fell back again into the mush on the ground.

"Get out of here," yelled Mrs. Crabtree. "And don't forget you owe me twenty-five dollars. I better get it by tomorrow night."

LC gulped. How could he forget? It was all he had been thinking about.

The Critter Kids spent the rest of the afternoon trying to train Yo Yo. He ran around the yard, barked at cars, chased butterflies, and did everything but listen.

"We better pray for a miracle tomorrow," said Gabby.

LC didn't say anything. He watched as Yo Yo ran around and around in circles, chasing his tail and barking.

"On second thought, a miracle may not even be enough," said Gabby.

LC just looked at Gabby. He couldn't help but think that maybe she was right.

CHAPTER 5

LEAVE IT TO YO YO!

The next day LC and the Critter Kids and Yo Yo got to the Critterville Dog Show just as it was about to begin. LC couldn't understand why everyone was dressed up.

"Handlers to the ring!" a voice announced.

"What does that mean?" asked LC.

Before anyone could answer, Su Su walked by with Princess. Su Su was dressed all in white with pink ribbons. Even Princess had pink ribbons in her fur.

"So, who's your handler?" Su Su asked.

"I am," said Gabby, grabbing the leash from LC. "Let's go, Yo Yo."

But Yo Yo wouldn't go.

Su Su laughed. "That dog will never win," Su Su said as she and Princess walked toward the ring.

"Maybe I should walk with Yo Yo," said LC.

"Okay," said Gabby. "But I'll show him in the ring."

"Only one minute to show time," the voice said over the intercom. "Handlers to the ring!"

"I guess this is it," said LC. "It's up to you, Yo Yo. You gotta do it. You gotta win the show."

But Yo Yo wasn't listening. He was watching Princess. He pulled LC toward the ring, and everyone else followed.

"Gimme the leash," said Gabby. "It's show time."

Gabby pulled Yo Yo into the ring. All the other dogs were already lined up. Gabby tried to lead Yo Yo to the end of the row, but he wouldn't budge. He wanted to sit next to Princess.

"Handlers, stand your dogs!" said a lady in a long dress with a diamond tiara on her head.

"Guess that's the judge," whispered Tiger to LC.

"Guess so," said LC.

Just then the judge turned around.

"Oh, no," said LC. "It's Mrs. Crabtree."

Mrs. Crabtree went over to the first dog, a Labrador retriever. It was standing perfectly straight with its head and tail

held high. Mrs. Crabtree walked down the line, carefully examining each dog. When she got to Yo Yo, she stopped. Yo Yo lay down and put his paws over his eyes. Gabby pulled on the leash and tried to get Yo Yo to stand, but he wouldn't move. Mrs. Crabtree shook her head and wrote something in her notebook.

"We don't have a chance," LC whispered to Gator.

Mrs. Crabtree continued to walk down the line, inspecting all the other dogs. When she finished, she made her way through the crowd to the judges' table.

"Handlers, walk your dogs around the ring," said Mrs. Crabtree.

Gabby put the leash in her left hand and yanked Yo Yo to her left side. She started to walk. But Yo Yo didn't want to walk on the left side. He pulled over to the right.

Mrs. Crabtree stood in the middle of the ring. The dogs walked in a circle around

her. Yo Yo kept moving to the right. Gabby kept pulling him back.

"He never walks on the left side," said LC to Tiger. "He always walks on the right."

Just then LC watched as Yo Yo pulled to the right and crossed in front of Gabby. She tripped over the leash and dropped it. Yo Yo ran to the middle of the ring, right smack into Mrs. Crabtree. She fell to the ground.

"This dog is disqualified," yelled Mrs. Crabtree. She dusted herself off and went to straighten her diamond tiara. But it wasn't there.

"Aaahhh!!!!!" screamed Mrs. Crabtree. "My tiara is gone! Someone has stolen my precious tiara!"

Yo Yo started barking and took off. All the other dogs started barking, too. Yo Yo ran across the ring. The other dogs broke loose and ran after Yo Yo.

"Let's go!" yelled LC to Tiger, Timothy, and Gator. "We've got to get Yo Yo."

They took off after Yo Yo and the other dogs. Everybody followed them. Yo Yo ran across the parking lot.

"What could Yo Yo be chasing?" Gabby asked LC.

LC just shrugged and kept on running.

When they turned the corner, there was Yo Yo. He had pinned a guy, who was all dressed up in a pin-striped suit, to the ground. And in Yo Yo's mouth was a brown paper bag.

LC and the Critter Kids ran over to Yo Yo and the guy in the suit.

"Yo Yo, get off," said LC. "And give me that bag."

All the other owners and their dogs gathered around them.

"That dog is a menace!" yelled Mrs.

Crabtree, shaking her finger at LC. "He ought to be sent to the pound."

"Really," said Su Su. "I told them that dog was no good."

"Get up right now and give me that bag," said LC.

Yo Yo wouldn't budge. LC grabbed one end of the bag and Yo Yo pulled on the other. Suddenly the bag ripped and out fell Mrs. Crabtree's diamond tiara. Everyone gasped.

"My tiara!" exclaimed Mrs. Crabtree.

Just then Sergeant Pokey appeared. He looked at the guy in the suit and at the tiara. "So, Whiskers," he said. "The gig is finally up."

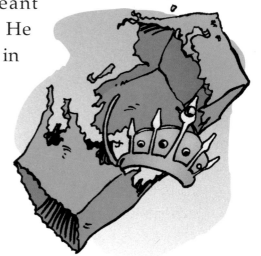

Whiskers got up slowly and

Sergeant Pokey handcuffed him. "What do you know, Whiskers, caught by a dog," the sergeant said. He turned to the crowd. "Who owns this dog?" he asked.

"I do," said LC.

"Your dog is a hero," the sergeant said. "We've been after the Critterville Cat Burglar for quite some time."

The sergeant handed LC twenty-five dollars. "Congratulations, son. Don't spend it all in one place."

LC turned to Mrs. Crabtree. "Here's the money I owe you," he said.

"That's okay," said Mrs. Crabtree. "Your dog found my tiara. You can keep the reward." Mrs. Crabtree bent down and patted Yo Yo on the head. He licked her face. Mrs. Crabtree laughed.

The Critter Kids all cheered.

Just then a newspaper reporter pushed his way through the crowd. "Line up with the dog so I can take your picture," he said

to LC and the Critter Kids. "You're front-page news, you know."

After he snapped the picture, everybody clapped. The reporter took out his notebook and walked over to LC. "Now that you're a hero, what do you have to say?"

LC thought for a minute and then he smiled. "Save your money for a rainy day," he said.

The Critter Kids laughed. LC patted Yo Yo on the head and Yo Yo licked his hand. "I always knew you were top dog," LC said to Yo Yo.